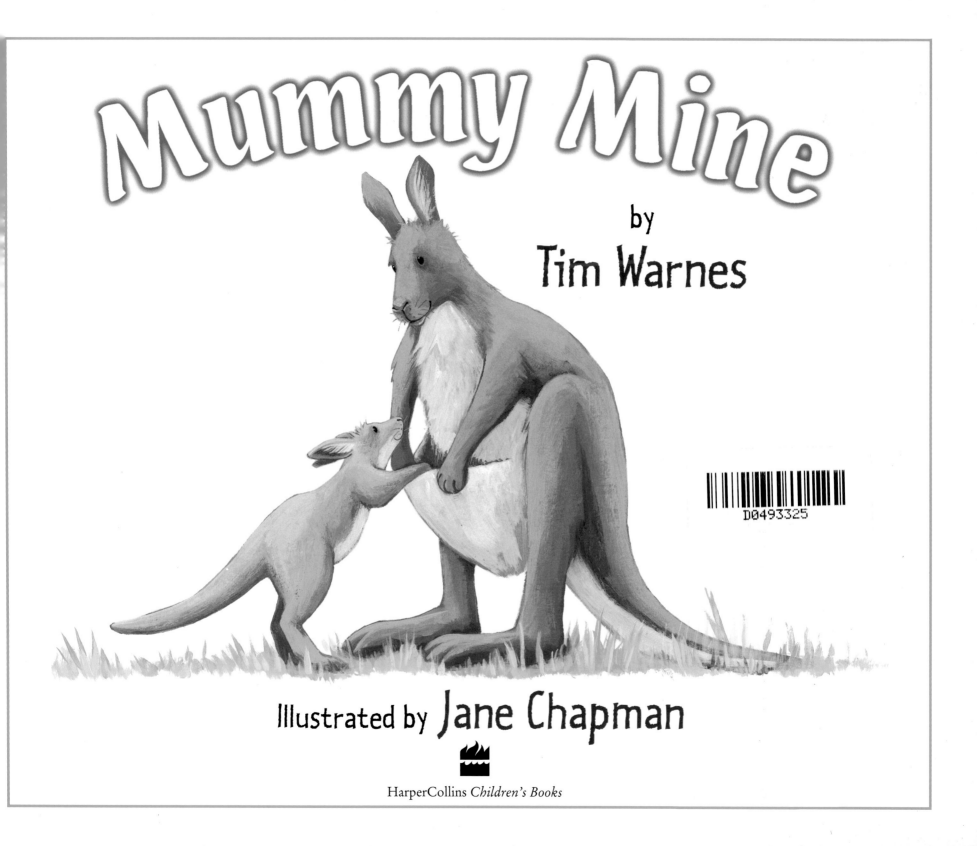

Mummy Mine

by
Tim Warnes

Illustrated by Jane Chapman

HarperCollins Children's Books

First published in hardback in the U.S.A. by HarperCollins Publishers Inc. in 2005
First published in paperback in Great Britain by HarperCollins Children's Books in 2006

1 3 5 7 9 10 8 6 4 2

ISBN-13: 978-0-00-721977-3
ISBN-10: 0-00-721977-6

HarperCollins Children's Books is a division of HarperCollins Publishers Ltd.

Text copyright © Tim Warnes 2005
Illustrations copyright © Jane Chapman 2005

Typography by Martha Rago

Visit our website at: www.harpercollinschildrensbooks.co.uk

Printed and bound in Hong Kong

For Mummy Cuddles

—T.W., J.C.

Mummy

huge

Mummy hairy

Mummy spiny

Mummy flutter

Mummy
tiny

pitter-patter

Mummy **LOUD**

Mummy STOMP

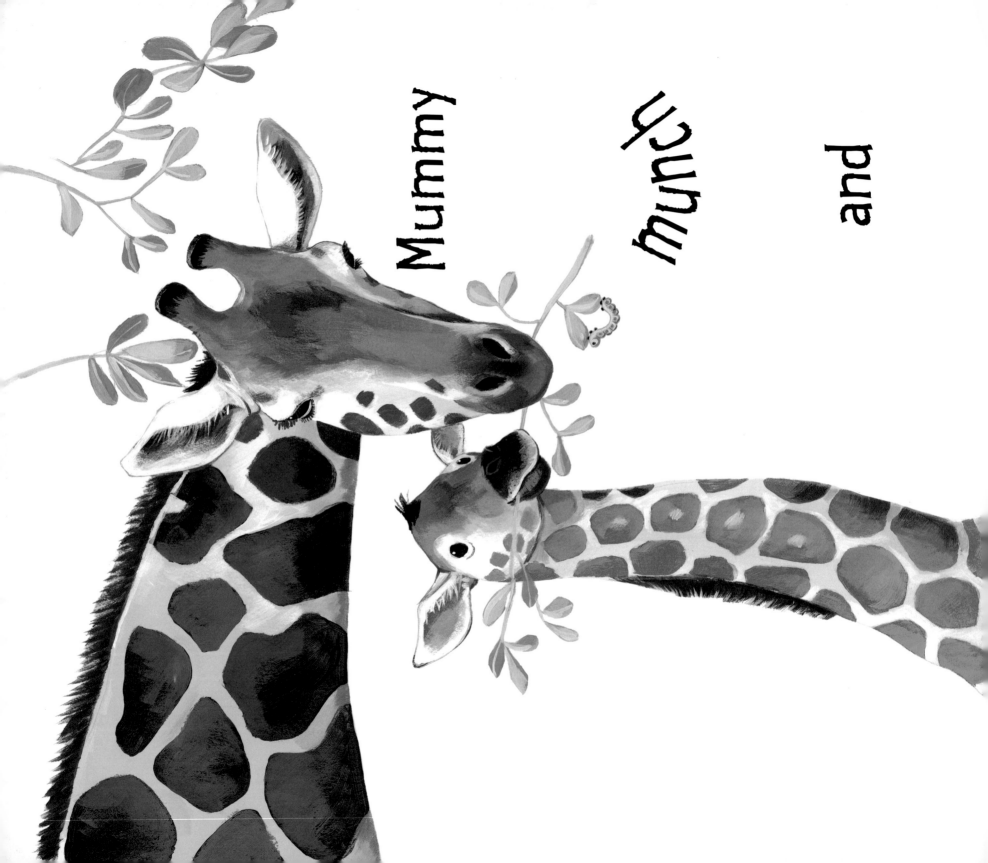

Mummy munch and

Mummy **full** Mummy **grubby**

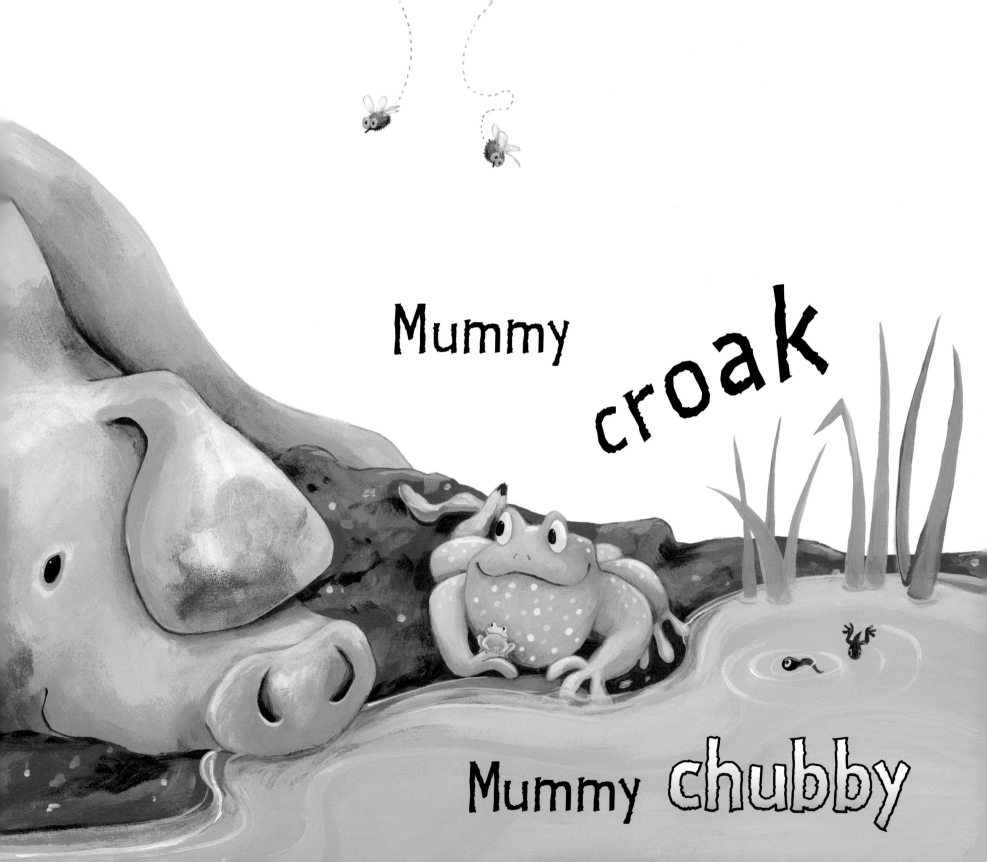

Mummy jump

Mummy funny

Icky-sticky
Mummy
honey

Mummy snoozing, Mummy lazy

clumsy Mummy –

whoopsy-daisy!

Mummy
noisy

Mummy
nosy

Mummy
carry

Mummy cosy.

Mummy cuddle on the vine,

Mummy kisses . . .

Mummy mine!